# CAPTAIN MARVEL

## CRAZY LIKE A FOX

Writer: Peter David
Pencils: Michael Ryan & Paul Azaceta
Colors: Chris Sotomoyor
Letters: Virtual Calligraphy's Cory Petit
Cover Artists: Chriscross, Howard Porter,
Neal Adams, Barry Kitson & Tom Flemming
Assistant Editors: Marc Sumerak & Nicole Wiley
Editor: Andy Schmidt

Collections Editor: Jeff Youngquist
Assistant Editor: Jennifer Grünwald
Book Designer: Julio Herrera

Editor in Chief: Joe Quesada
Publisher: Dan Buckley

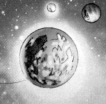

# PREVIOUSLY

Captain Marvel, half-breed son of the like-named late Kree hero, possesses vast cosmic powers which are governed through the nega-bands he wears upon his wrists. Unfortunately, one of those powers — cosmic awareness — so overwhelmed him that it drove him mad. His erratic actions and mindset make him extremely dangerous.

He is molecularly and mentally bonded to professional sidekick and musician Rick Jones. Through prearranged agreement, they switch places every twenty-four hours, with one residing in "our" universe while the other exists in the sub-atomic Microverse.

Rick endeavors to keep Captain Marvel in line with his "Psi-Fry" ability in which he can inflict great mental pain upon the Captain. However, employing this power takes a great toll on Rick, and he must use it judiciously lest he do himself permanent damage.

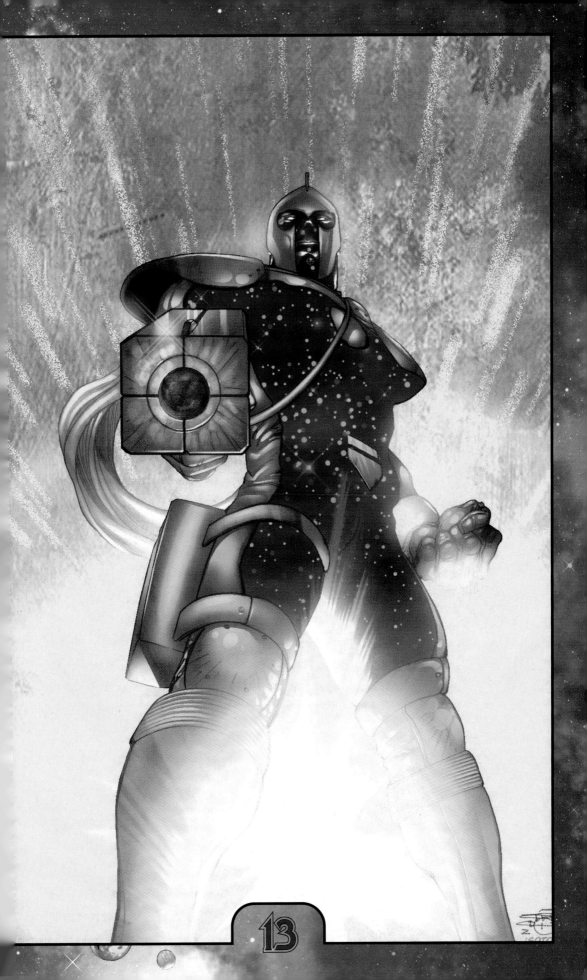

13

Unhhh! You mongrel!

Well...yes. What's your point?

Get off me!!

In a minute.

This is none of your affair!

Technically, it's not--unfff-- yours either.

You'd allied yourself with the Kree. Yet now you're acting on behalf of the Badoon. Which leads one to conclude the Kree and Badoon are joining forces.

Wha--? How...did you know?!

Ohhh, you'd be amazed what I know, Burstaar.

Doubtless you remember me from our previous encounter in the Negative Zone. Remember how I acted. How I moderated my powers. Tried to incapacitate rather than kill.

But things have changed. I've changed. It's time you knew...

Is...is he *dead?* Is--

You *killed* him?

Yes.

No. He was too terrified to face me, so he snapped his own neck.

Happens *all* the time.

You *jest,* of course!

It's either that, or kill *you* next.

And again that *stunning* sense of humor!

You just keep *telling* yourself that.

I am Magister Pop, and on behalf of--

Magister... we need to speak.

But I'm busy *congratulating* our savior!

We must have *ceremonies!* He must be *feted* and--!

Magister, *please!* It is of the *utmost* urgency!

My advisors *insist* on my attention. Affairs of state. *You* know how it is.

Of course.

I'll be but a moment.

Take your time.

Now what is so damnably important that--

Magister, this...Captain Marvel...he is infamous.

Nonsense! He is a great Kree hero!

No, Magister! That was the *father*. This is the *son*.

He is *insane*! Driven *mad* with power! He's conquered *worlds*, assaulted entire races!

There is no telling what his true motivations or plans could be!

A...madman you say? Are you sure...?

Beyond question, Magister.

We may have traded *one* menace for an even *greater* one.

...ell...! *Captain Marvel!* Our world and I owe you a debt of gratitude. One that can never truly be repaid.

I didn't do it seeking your *gratitude,* Magister. I sensed Burstaar would be here, and could not allow him to succeed in his venture. It's as *simple* as that.

However, if you offer your gratitude, I accept it freely.

Then it is given... freely.

Farewell.

These were the actions of a madman?

Our intelligence reports were *very* thoro--

*Idiots!* I see no evidence of intelligence, of *any* sort.

Enough of this. We will reconvene tomorrow and determine the fate of the Kahfan.

May your advice be more *sound* on the morrow.

Good night, Magister.

Sleep well, Magister.

Yes, yes, goodnight.

I simply do not comprehend it.

How could they have led me *so* astray?

No wonder it's impossible to understand the ingratitude of the Kahfan. I can scarcely credit the thinking of my *own* advisors.

What is the world coming to?

Do you want me to answer that?

Wha--?!?!

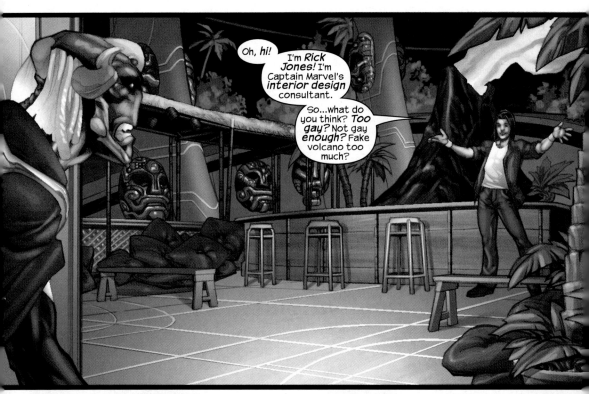

Oh, *hi!* I'm *Rick Jones!* I'm Captain Marvel's *interior design* consultant.

So...what do you think? *Too gay?* Not gay *enough?* Fake volcano too much?

You're supposed to be guards! You idiots! You nobodies! *What am I paying you people for?!?*

Magister, *no one* went in or out, we *swear!*

Gotta admit, we *didn't* have a lot of time to work. But Marv, he can be a real *piston* when he puts his mind to it.

Mostly I made the suggestions. But he was the one who got it done.

You'd be amazed how much you can accomplish when using dimensional folds and--

Kill this creature!

14

Marv.

The babe's name is Marv?

Marv! This has *you* written all over it! Come on, Marv! I *know* you can hear me! What's this latest game about?

Who's this *"Marv"* you're talkin' to, pal? Look, enough's enough. You got *any* idea *who* it is you're trying to yank around here?

Of *course* I do chowderhead! Over there...that's one *Rick Jones*, teenage idiot who snuck out onto the testing range of a gamma bomb just to prove he wasn't chicken to some idiots so *inconsequential* that he won't remember their names ten years later.

And you... you're *also* Rick Jones, a couple years later, when Captain America took you on as his partner and dressed you in his dead sidekick's uniform...a move that, in retrospect, could be seen as *disturbingly* necrophilic.

Hey! Who the *heck* do you think you ar--

I made an interesting discovery today. Remember when I helped Entropy re-create the universe?

Yeaaahhh...

Well, it wasn't exactly a *seamless* job.

I mean, that should have been *obvious*, right? Considering I'm still in the Kree costume I acquired in a timeline that supposedly no longer *happened*.

*Whoooaaa!* There's maybe a million chicks camped out out there! All colors! All shapes!

They're groupies. I'm a rock star here.

*Awwwright!* How do I get *down* there?

*I'd* be glad to *throw* him down.

*That's* an option, if you'd *all* care to die.

Marv! For cryin' out loud...!

All right, all right...

There are a few..."time rips," for want of a better term, in the universe's fabric.

You mean like in "*Time Bandits*," with dwarves jumping through time?

No. More like temporal fault lines. I've found that by *stimulating* them with cosmically-charged photonic particles...which I can generate via the nega-bands...

...I can *really* shake things up. Fo starters, I can cau people to come fac to-face with their own past selves. It's fun.

How in *hell* is it *fun*?!

...you've always moped about how, because of your foolish teen behavior, you caused so much hardship for so many.

So here's your chance to set it right.

That's it, girls! Form a *human mattress*! Then I'll--

All you need do is convince your earliest self *not* to sneak out onto the testing facility.

Aw *no* you don't!

Hey!

Uh-huh. And if I do?

Why, isn't it *obvious*? If you *do*...

...you get to live a normal life. So does *Bruce Banner*.

For that matter, so does Betty Ross. And Marlo. Jen Walters Jim Wilson, Jarella. The list is *endless*.

That's all I have to do?

That's all. Now if you'll excuse me...

...I have my *own* concerns to attend to.

Shi'ar Ale. Practically toxic to non-Shi'ar, as I recall.

You recall right. This stuff'll take the carbon-scoring off your hull.

So just what kind of hallucination am I *having?*

The painful kind.

OOOOFFF!

*Grozit,* you didn't have to *do* that!

What is your *problem,* anyway?

Because I can tell you right now, if the Kree High Command sent you to--

Oh.

Do you *understand* now?

Yes. Yes, I...well, I sort of...

No. No, not *really.* Not at all.

For someone who's cosmically aware, you're *distressingly* clueless.

Oh... my God. It's... The... the pain...the insanity...so much... ...*too much*...I...

I...I thought...

You thought you could *handle* cosmic awareness.

Yes.

You thought you could be a force for *good.* A *hero,* like your father.

Yes.

Instead you fail utterly. You descend into madness. You care about *nothing* and *no one.* Faced with power and nigh-immortal, you devise ways to kill time entertainingly until it ends.

Yes.

You could end it *sooner.*

H-How...?

Kill *him.*

He's a drunken reprobate. An embarrassment. *None* will miss him.

Kill him... and it *all* goes away.

*You* get it, right? I mean, you've seen *tons* more than the Beav here.

You know what's out there. What lurks in the shadows or under rocks. You know this ain't a dream. You slapped me around to prove it.

Yeah, I think I know the score.

Want me to slap *him* around?

No, I want you to talk *sense* into him.

Into him? Or into you?

What's *that* supposed to mean?

I mean, are you nuts? Trying to talk him out of...

Jeez! Can you imagine a world without you in it?

By *"you,"* I mean the Rick Jones that's the hero, the adventurer, the go-to guy when things get *rough!* Not the teenage jerk harmonica player.

Maybe *you're* the one who's trippin'. My God, the lives I ruined with one stupid act--

And what about the lives you *saved*, huh?

What about the times the Hulk saved the planet...?

...or trashed entire cities?

Or beat back alien invasions?

Or put other heroes in the hospital?

I mean, c'mon, man! How am I supposed to take you seriously? *Look* at you! It's embarrassing!

The ultimate super hero *wannabe!*

Yeah? Well at least I wanna be *something!*

How about *you*, hotshot? What do *you* wanna be, huh?

Left alone.

Well, then...I guess you helped create the right monster, after all.

≶Hiiiiic≶
≶urrrrrrp≶

See? He's dead drunk. Just one squeeze takes out the drunk part.

No.

No? How can you not want to? Seeing where it leads, the destination...

Now you're the one who's naïve.

I'm on a hero's journey, "Captain." It may lead to you... but I don't believe you're the destination.

You see... bottom line, you're no different than him. Both drunks: him on *alcohol,* you on power. The abuse remains. Only the *substance* changes.

What sort of hero's journey winds up with the hero the same as when he started?

Is it... Is it really that bad? All the stuff that happens, I mean?

It will be if you play like that. God, you suck. Here, lemme show you.

I thought "Rolling Stone" said you were no good.

Maybe, but I suck less than you. Now watch...

Pick up the gun. Pick it up and *end* this farce.

*You* pick it up. *You* use it, if you're so godly.

But you won't...because, bottom line, you're afraid.

You know you're not the last stop in the journey.

You don't want *me* to end it before I become *you*. *You* want to end it before you become something *else*. Something so much *better* than *you*, it's terrifying you.

As I walk away from you, you want to run from it.

The thing is, *I'm* not scared. Are *you*?

No. Because I'm holding the gun.

Then use it. But *spare* us the pseudo-god crock of--

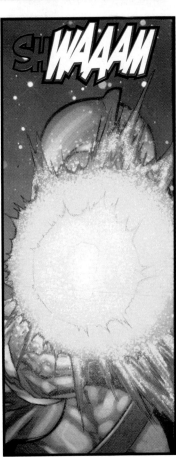

SHWAAAM

These are his parents: Elysius of Titan, who used their technology and clone material from the late Captain Mar-Vell to create "Genis." Unfortunately, Elysius has since passed as well.

If they're both deceased, then the Kree become responsible for him!

On what grounds?!

He's been seen wearing a Kree captain's uniform!

Well, perhaps he'll start sporting ugly pointed ears and we'll say he's your problem!

That's enough! Back to your places immediately!

The Kree must be sanctioned! In addition to supporting the terrorist activities of Captain Marvel...

...we have learned they've formed an alliance with the Badoon! A race so warlike, so vile, they're not even a member of this council!

We are not unaware of the enmity between Kree and Skrull that could cause such charges to be made without foundation.

Still, at the risk of getting off track, they bear investigation. We of the Shi'ar call upon the Kree to *answer*.

We have offered philanthropic aid to the Badoon, yes. They are a downtrodden, misunderstood race, seeking to better themselves.

It is simply our desire to ennoble them. To lift them up to the level of other, more civilized races, such as the princely Skrulls.

Your sarcasm is as pathetic as your lies.

Fellow beings, we have *visuals!* Visuals of the Badoon massing on a secret base on Tau Ceti IV. Training with Kree aid, Kree weaponry and Kree soldiers overseeing it all.

They intend to use the Badoon as footsoldiers in new realms of conquest.

*See!* See for yourself the unholy alliance of--!

Pama!

Eh?

Not exactly as advertised, is it, Skrull?

And guess who's going to go next. I spy with *my* cosmic eye, something that starts with... *"dead."*

Be seeing you.

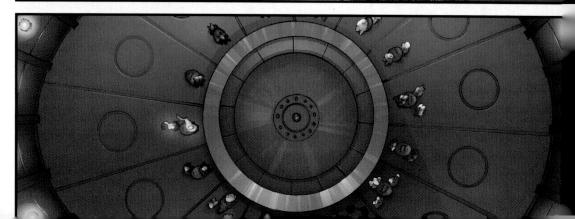

The threat is over!

We *did* it!

*You* did it? Clearly the firepower of our Skrullcruisers provided the--

Be quiet.

--difference in the--

Do you *never* tire of hearing yourself--

A plague on *all* of you, I said *be quiet!!*

It was too easy!

You call that easy?

It took the *combined fire power* of our fleets!

We threw everything we had at him to stop him!

WATHAAM!

I believe that was the speaker's *point*.

Hello.

Don't get up.

Good to see you.

If I don't kill you, have a nice day.

So. Have I lived up to my advance *billing?*

To think that whatever deities there *are* would put so much power into so unstable, so unworthy a vessel.

You may well be right. Then again, Voltaire—a member of the human race that you so despise—may have put it most aptly.

"God is a comedian playing to an audience too afraid to laugh."

Depending on your comfort level, think of me then as God...

...or God's opening act.

Now hear me! You think I presented a problem to you? That's nothing compared to the problem *you're* going to present to the rest of the galaxy!

What is he *talking* about? This is an out--

FWAAM

His next word was going to be *"rage."*

Anyone *else* care to have their next word completed by me?

Anyone at all? No? Pity.

Now then...

I am cosmically aware. That means, among other things, I see the threads of the future and the many ways they can interweave.

And there is one *very* consistent pattern when I look at your threads.

In the future, all of you will form a genuine alliance. *All* differences will be set aside.

Rather than this council being a place to air grievances, it will instead be a united front.

Ally with the Skrulls? Those treacherous... It will never happen!

As hard as it is to believe, I assure you it will be so.

But then...why act so *threateningly* if you present good news?

It's not good news. See, once united...

"You *conquer* the galaxy.

"All with the best of intentions, of course. Conquerors always have those. The bloody result is the same, and the bodies are stacked three high.

"You achieve absolute power...which corrupts absolutely. Believe me..."

I'm the expert on that.

So I'm going to save the galaxy by annihilating *all* you future conquerors.

You have a week to get your affairs in order, and then, like bugs...

Squish.

Questions? Comments?

The spokeswoman from the Shi'ar. I believe *you* have something to say.

I do, actually...at the risk of being vaporized.

By all means, risk it.

In considering the matter of your actions--your conquests, your attacks, your wars, your trespasses--we've taken into account the fact that, in addition to being half-Kree...

...you're also half-Titan.

And you've summoned my late mother's side of the family?

I thought you might.

Cosmically aware, remember?

Then you're aware they're here, I suppose.

Oh yes. And of course, true to their names...

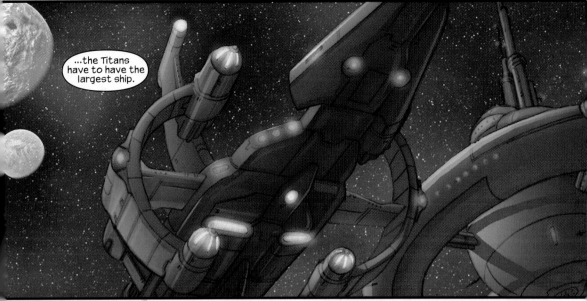

...the Titans have to have the largest ship.

It will make no difference.

Let them send my uncle, Eros, to chastise me. Or Mentor, or Thena. Hell, bring on *Thanos* if he's so inclined.

I promise you, nothing is--

Genis.

Genis... it's enough.

This... this is... ...it's a trick.

It's no trick.

*Yes, it is!!!*

Genis, put down the gun. Now.

Whoever... whatever you are... don't move.

Or I swear to God I'll *kill* you.

It's a relief to hear you say that. Here you seemed to believe *you* were God.

*Shut up!* Don't tell me what I believe!

Why--

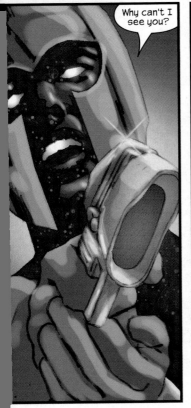

Why can't I see you?

See me? Genis, darling...I'm *right here*.

No. I mean my cosmic awareness...it... it should have...

You! Take it off. Right now.

"*It?*" My outfit? You want me *naked?*

Genis, even for *you*, that's wandering into a weird area.

*Koff*
*Koffff*

Now I ask you...

...is *that* how you show respect for your mother?

Oh, don't look so surprised. Did you truly think Titan science couldn't develop force shields sufficient to withstand anything you might throw at us?

This day was inevitable, Genis, and we've had plenty of time to consider all the possibilities.

Really.

Consider *this*, then.

*You* put them up to this, didn't you?

Even from beyond the grave, father, you come up with new and interesting ways to make my life more miserable than it already is.

What the devil do you want from me, eh?

Here lies Captain Mar-Vell of Kree-Lar

I should have just destroyed the whole Titan ship right then.

And then blown up the council chamber. See how much good her shields do when she's floating in space.

Why didn't I do that? Why?

Because you were confused. You were caught off guard, and that's a sensation you've *forgotten* about. It paralyzed your thought process.

Who *knows* what sort of evil schemes he's currently engaged in?

"Evil schemes?" My dear council, Genis is not evil. He's deeply troubled.

With all respect, Titaness, the two are *not* mutually exclusive. When we asked Titan to send a representative, we were expecting...

More force and less nurturing?

I am what I *am*, Council-woman.

And what precisely would that *be*, Titaness? Our intelligence stated that you were dead.

"Kree intelligence." *There's* a contradiction in terms.

*Shut up*, Skrull! No one *asked* you!

At the risk of providing more fodder for Kree/Skrull bickering, we had also heard reports that you had been killed.

The reports, Councilwoman, were *greatly* exaggerated.

For the record, he's mostly slaughtered Kree and their misbegotten allies, the Badoon. The Skrull Empire has no objection to *those* activities.

Indeed. But the threat your son poses is *no* exaggeration.

He promises wholesale slaughter, and he's engaged in such activities already...

And when he comes for you, Skrull? Then what?

Perhaps *we* will *not* be such easy pickings as you and yours.

Or perhaps they will. Perhaps they all will. He mowed through our fleet as if we were nothing.

Take your nurturing approach, Elysius, if you feel it viable.

But we will *not* wait to be victims of genocide.

If this matter is not settled to our satisfaction in three days...

...we will come after him.

And *you.* And that's the naked truth.

My. That was cosmic.

Then again, I'm sure you hear that a lot.

Captain?

What's wrong?

I miss Rick. I didn't think I would, but I do.

I miss his scolding, and his attitude, and his humanity.

It was so easy to feel *superior* when he was around.

Having the power of a god should be enough to make you feel superior in any event.

You'd *think* that, wouldn't you?

So what are you going to do about it?

I don't know.

Bring him back to *life*, I guess.

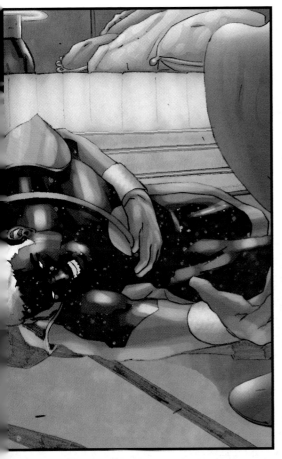

They *threatened* us? The *nerve!*

I'm starting to wonder whether Genis doesn't have the right idea about them. How dare they treat my sister in that fashion! Of all the--

Eros, not *everything* need be about you.

Not for lack of trying.

I'll grant you that.

The point is, we have to focus on Genis now. We've put it off as long as we can.

We've put it off because it would mean explaining your presence here. We weren't sure if he's *ready* for it.

Well, as his--and his father's--beloved humans are wont to say...

...ready or *not*, here we *come.*

Seems whacked that Mr. Cosmic Know-It-All is coming to me for answers.

You know, Rick, it didn't really sink in the first twenty times you said that, but the twenty-first was the keeper.

Okay, okay. So...it could be a clone of your mother. That'd be a cakewalk for them, right?

Yes. Go on.

Could be an evil twin. Or a parallel dimension being. Hell, maybe she's left over from that time rift thing you opened.

Here's what I keep coming back to, though...

...why would any of those options have thwarted my cosmic awareness? Could it have something to do with your *brother*?

Uhm...if I have a bro', Marv, it's news to me.

Anyhoo, I'm thinking we won't get it sorted out here. Best way is to go to the source.

We've tracked his photonic discharge, Eros. He's half a klarn away.

If I'm not mistaken, that's where his father is buried.

Believe me, you're *not* mistaken.

We've got a visual *lock* on him, sir.

What's he doing?

I'm not sure. It...

It appears to be some sort of *greeting*.

He's powering up to fire on us!

Target and fire first.

Eros! But why--?

Before one can discipline young ones, dear sister, one has to show willingness to be firm.

Firing *main battery!*

What the--?

Some sort of light image of him!

The little cretin tricked us!

He likes to play games. Takes after his uncle Eros in that regard.

Not funny, Elysius.

Helm. Track him.

Sir...if his course stays consistent...

He's heading *home*, sir.

"He's heading for Titan."

"Welcome to my world, Rick. Or...more precisely... welcome to yours.

"It's an age-old question, isn't it. If you could go back in time, knowing what you know now, and smother Hitler in his crib...*would* you?

"Well, I do know what I know now. And here it is, for your enlightenment. The mightiest races in the galaxy, truly joining forces. Not simply as a bickering council...but to act for the 'greatest good of sentient beings'...

"...meaning, of course, themselves.

Ever heard of Marcus Tullius Cicero, Rick? Famed Roman orator. He stated, "Let the punishment match the offense."

The offense of Terrans is that they live. How does that warrant such a punishment? And they call *me* insane.

They call you insane, Marv, because you *are* insane.

Not long ago, you went on about how we're friends. Then you took control of my mind and caused me to fall to my death.

But I brought you back. Do you know why?

Because nature has no love for solitude, and always leans, as it were, on some support; and the sweetest support is found in the most intimate friendship.

Cicero said that as well.

That's 'cause Cicero never had you for a friend.

I'm like this puppet on your *strings*, Marv. I stew down here in the Microverse and you yank me around. How'm I supposed to live like this?

Y'know what? Forget about it.

Get us to Titan, sort this thing out with your mother...

...and *then* we stop War of the Worlds, Part II, no matter how far in the future it may be.

Speaker... may we address you privately for a moment...?

Well, *this* is a shocking development. Kree and Skrull, side by side?

Speaker...in case you've forgotten, our council deliberations are broadcast live to our respective empires.

A certain amount of, uhm...

Posturing?

Yes, exactly. *Thank* you.

Don't mention it.

Some posturing is necessary to keep our constituents satisfied.

In point of fact, however, our truly important work transpires behind closed doors, where civil tongues accomplish far more than belligerence.

I could not agree more. So what brings you here?

We gave the Titans three days to deal with Captain Marvel.

We're thinking...that may have been overly generous.

What would you propose?

Attack.

Now.

You called it, Mother. He's here.

I'm ready to do whatever it takes.

And you *have* what it takes, my dear. Remember...you're the *new* Captain Marvel now.

Just so long as I get to kick his butt while I'm doing all that.

Do justice to the name that your brother has tragically disgraced... but show the mercy he has been lacking.

I should *never* have let her start monitoring earth television. It's a bad influence.

Don't be that way. Besides, you've been monitoring it as well, and it hasn't affected you.

Oh, fine. What *ever*.

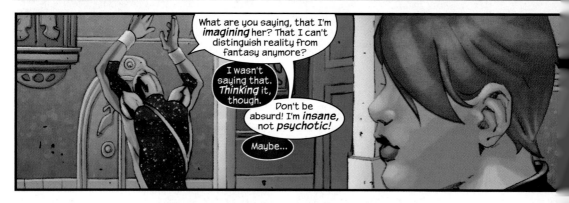

Man, I was gonna use the psi-fry to rein you in...but your sister seems like she can handle herself.

She's... *not* my sister!

Then why did you act like she is?

Because she is! It's...I don't know! Nothing's making sense!

Marv, this is no time to *flake* out on me! Well...not *more* flaked out than you've *been*! Not if Earth's really hanging in the balance, like you said!

Don't listen to him. You are a god in the midst of humanity.

Last time humanity thought they had one of those, they *crucified* him. So what do he and his kind know of such things?

I...know, Epiphany, but... it's all...

Marv! Epiphany's *not there!* You're *imagining* it!

Captain, if they destroy your confidence...if they destroy you...then Earth's annihilation is assured.

Shut up...both of you...

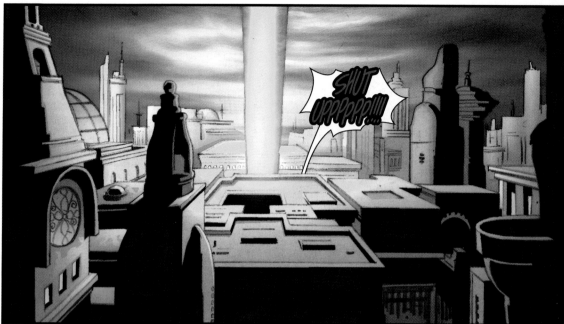

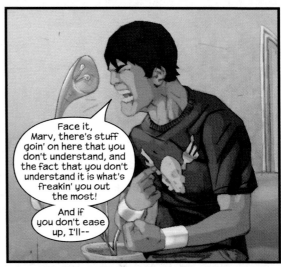

Second...since your own recollections seem dicey, maybe you want to sit down and talk with this Elysius.

And why would I want to do that?

'Cause maybe she *IS* your mother! You once had a vision of your future in which she'd returned, remember?

Yes. Yes... I remember. I remember everything.

Genis, listen to me. Listen carefully.

The rest of the Titans... they're...

Out of phase, yes, I know. Afraid to face me...

No. Not afraid to face you.

Afraid of hurting you.

We care about you. All of us.

I know this is all very confusing, but there's an explanation...

They're just trying to confuse you.

It's all right. I know what I have to do now.

Oh, I am *not* liking the sound of that.

You see, the universe... it's...not quite put together right.

There are temporal rifts that are causing--

Leaks, yes, of Chronal energy.

I know. I was *responsible* for them. They're located at various points throughout reality. There's one just off Proxima Centauri...another in Tau Ceti...one I closed up over on Earth's moon...

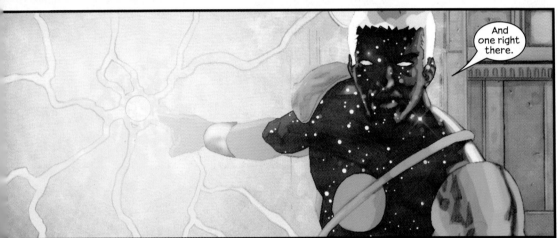

And one right there.

Genis! What are you *doing*?!?

Isn't it *obvious*, Mother? I'm sending you and loving Sis here back to whatever unreal, path-not-taken wrinkle in time you've come from.

Genis, no!!!

18

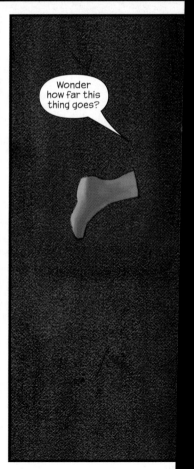

It's almost like reliving birth.

Except my birth is a lie, of course. No mother's womb for me.

I was a test tube genetic cocktail, just like my sister...

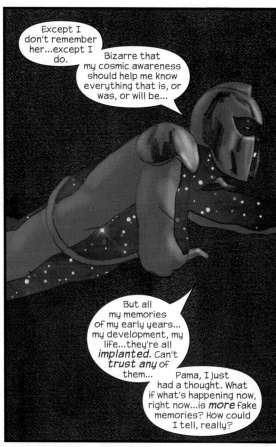

Except I don't remember her...except I do.

Bizarre that my cosmic awareness should help me know everything that is, or was, or will be...

But all my memories of my early years... my development, my life...they're all *implanted*. Can't *trust any* of them...

Pama, I just had a thought. What if what's happening now, right now...is *more* fake memories? How could I tell, really?

It seems as vivid, as real, as anything I now know to be false.

What if I don't exist at all? What if I'm just a rough draft program for memories yet to be implanted in--

Ah. Looks like a way out.

I swear, though, if someone hauls me out, holds me upside down and tries to slap my behind, I'm going to--

Ladeeez and gentlemen--! Please direct your attention to the far end of the Big Tent!

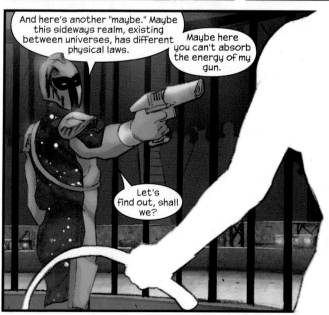

What you don't get, Genis, is that we're here to help you.

It's a piece of genuine *luck* you brought us here.

Or maybe it's not luck. Maybe you sensed that only someplace like *here* could you be made to listen to reason.

*Eros!* What are you do--?!

This is an example of the area known as "N-th Space." We are, literally, neither here nor there. But for someone of your considerable power capabilities, it's the only arena where we can handle you.

Don't be so sure of that.

I'm *Captain Marvel,* Eros. I am a mad god.

I grew up with a mad god, Genis. I *knew* a mad god. A mad god was a friend of mine.

Genis, you are *no* mad god.

Oh *really?* Then what *am* I?

A let-down.

Please direct your attention heavenward for the moment we had to call...

...the *mother* of all confrontations!

Genis...we should have come to you sooner. We bear some responsibility in all this.

But it took the greatest minds in Titan much musing, research and meditation to divine what had happened.

Until we knew for certain, we didn't want to approach you. That was a *mistake*.

I think you'll find your major mistake was approaching me now.

Whoever you *are*, or obviously hope I'll *think* you are--

You saved me. In this universe, you brought me back from a realm of the dead through an epic quest combining science and magic in ways previously undreamed of.

You did it because you could not *stand* the injustice of my untimely passing.

That never happened.

Yes, it did. But not to *you*.

Huh?

In this universe... you already existed. But you were *different*. More heroic, more capable, right from the start. In fact, in this reality your "creation" was such a success that I was inspired to repeat the process that bore you to produce a sister for you.

I suppose, on some level, you couldn't help but produce an idealized version of yourself.

But then you yourself entered this reality...and, in so doing, automatically *replaced* yourself.

Like a pebble in a pond, this action caused waves of "discontinuity." The rips in space, such as the rift you pulled us through...

"...and other shifts in the space time continuum, including having the same person be in different places in the same reality. But each reality is equally 'real,' existing side by side."

You must have noticed the discontinuity in your own life. Wearing the Kree uniform...Rick Jones' status as music idol in the Microverse...even though technically neither event occurred.

The universe is continuing to pick and choose, sort matters out. It's *healing* itself.

And now it's time to heal you.

Get away from me.

No.

Do you see, Genis? Do you understand at last?

You were *never* insane. Confused, frustrated, and understandably so...but not insane. You comprehended your actions the entire time.

You were just looking to avoid growing up...like Peter Pan.

You enjoyed having all the powers that your station in life granted you...

...but you didn't want the *responsibilities.* You wanted to do whatever you felt like...and saying you were crazy enabled you to have it both ways.

But *really,* you wanted someone to set limits. To rein you in. To tell you, "No. Enough."

Rick developed the ability to hurt you mentally because you subconsciously told him how to do it.

But that wasn't *sufficient,* was it.

You made your endeavors bigger and bigger until you posed such a threat that your very *existence* was threatened.

No! I *am* insane! I don't care about you... about the universe...about anything...and by the way, I'm *not* threatened. I could take on the Shi'ar, the Kree...

Yes. You could. But *not* we Titans. We made you...

...and we can *break* you.

≥Urkh≤

I'd like to tell you this will hurt me more than you...but that's really *not* true.

M-Mother... no...

It's poetic justice, dear. If you truly are crippled in mind, as you claim to be...

I don't get it. What just happened?

I saw them get hauled into that weird glowy rift and then, like, seconds later, out they--

Oh, it was far more than *seconds.*

Really? 'Cause it seemed like--

Wait...you can see me? Hear me?

Of course. I am Mentor, leader of the Titans.

I thought *Robin* was leader of the Titans.

Shut up.

Yessir.

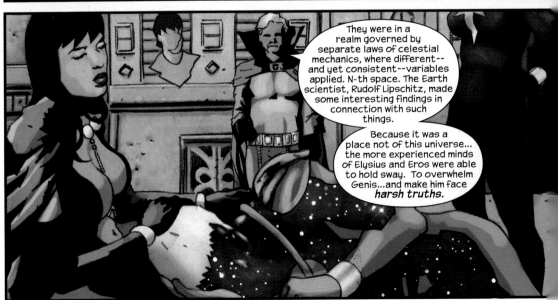

They were in a realm governed by separate laws of celestial mechanics, where different-- and yet consistent--variables applied. N-th space. The Earth scientist, Rudolf Lipschitz, made some interesting findings in connection with such things.

Because it was a place not of this universe... the more experienced minds of Elysius and Eros were able to hold sway. To overwhelm Genis...and make him face *harsh truths.*

"His inability to handle his cosmic awareness stemmed purely from his immaturity. All others who have this gift have a lifetime of experience to help them handle it.

"Genis *ran* from it. Abused it. Couldn't handle it.

"Now..."

Now what? Now we're supposed to believe he can handle it?

He remains a *threat!*

The Kree and Skrull speak true, if *gratingly.*

Our combined armada encircles this world. Do you truly wish to match your might against ours, Mentor? Would you defend this...lunatic?

We will do what is necessary to protect a potential force for good.

Leave him to us. We will *help* him. *Guide* him...

I'm afraid, Mentor, that may not be good enough...

Then perhaps...this will...

Genis, no! What are you doing--?

I know this will sound strange coming from me, Mother, but...

...trust me.

END.

# MARVELS

## 10TH ANNIVERSARY EDITION

**MARVEL**®

# CELEBRATE 10 YEARS OF MARVELS!

## KURT BUSIEK • ALEX ROSS